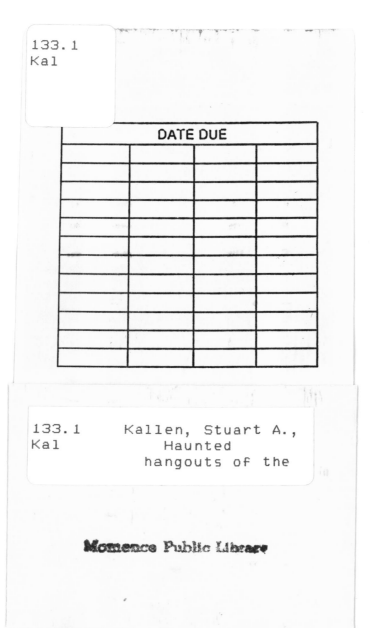

# HAUNTED HANGOUTS

*Written by Stuart A. Kallen*

Published by Abdo & Daughters, 6535 Cecilia Circle, Edina, Minnesota 55439.

Library bound edition distributed by Rockbottom Books, Pentagon Tower, P.O. Box 36036, Minneapolis, Minnesota 55435.

Library of Congress Number: 91-073065          ISBN: 1-56239-036-8
Inside Illustrations by: Tim Blough
Cover Illustration by: Tim Blough
Inside Photos by: Stuart Kallen

**Edited by: Rosemary Wallner**

# TABLE OF CONTENTS

*It is said that ghosts haunt the ancient castles of England.*

# GHOSTS OF STONE

They stand alone, the ghosts of stone. Some upon high, craggy cliffs. Some in deserted windswept fields. Some in deep forest glens. They can be found in almost every town, city, and village. Haunted houses, churches, theaters, and castles — here are where the phantoms live.

Some are made of fieldstone, some of timber and others of brick. The undead spirits cling to their rotting walls like fungus. Some have been abandoned for years, their broken windows reminding passing travelers of gaping eye sockets in a colossal skull. Should some innocent wanderer enter these haunted sanctuaries, they will smell the foul corruption and hear the restless groans of the undead.

Many haunted houses are occupied by the living. The merry tinkle of life goes on while the specters of long-dead cadavers wander the worm-eaten halls. Perhaps a teen-ager lives in the house. They might be a prime target for a poltergeist, who could suck the young person's life energy and use it for ghoulish destruction. Many ghosts haunt places where they died days, years, or centuries ago. Violent death, unfinished business, revenge — these are but a few reasons why phantoms restlessly wander. They return once a year, once every ten years, or maybe every night. Replaying the moment of their death: the bride who was murdered on her wedding night; the soldier who died in a castle's torture chamber; the wife who was bricked into a wall by her demented husband; the senile king, long dead, still looking for his throne. They announce their arrival with doors and windows slamming, pictures flying off the wall, armor clanking, moans, and shrieks. The phantoms don't care what the living think, but those of us who are living can only run in mortal terror.

# CHAPTER 1
# HAUNTED AMERICA

Most Americans think of their country as the most modern, up-to-date place on the Earth. While that may be true, there is also a hidden America. A supernatural America full of haunted houses, poltergeists, ghost ships, ghouls, phantoms, and specters. America is haunted from the giant cities in the East, to the industrial Midwest, across the sweeping plains and into the mountains and forests of the West. From the Atlantic to the Pacific, people tell stories of spirits, sprites, pixies, hobgoblins, imps, ogres, demons, and gnomes. It's enough to make your hair stand on end, your blood curdle, and your flesh crawl.

If you want to visit the haunted places where you live, a trip to your local library or bookstore could turn up a wealth of information about nearby hauntings. There are many books that contain exact addresses of ghostly hangouts in almost every state. From north to south, from east to west, petrifying cases of the supernatural reach out and haunt someone.

# TWO CENTURIES OF GHOSTS

To get to the old Millfield Inn, one must cross the Sunday River on a covered bridge that was built in 1874. Then, travel across the railroad tracks where thousands of coal trains have chugged past, blowing their high, lonesome whistles into the gloomy night.

The Millfield Inn now stands alone and abandoned. Its sagging roof shelters only rats, bats, and ghosts. But once upon a time, the inn was the hub of life in the Ohio Valley. Built in 1811, in the town of Millfield, Ohio, the inn housed many weary travelers making their way through the Southern Ohio wilderness. They could always count on a warm fire, a hot meal, and a strong drink when they stayed at the inn. Some say that George Washington slept there, but that was before the hauntings started.

The Millfield Inn is built on a foundation of massive hickory trees laid across the basement. In the early 1800s ancient hickory and ash trees covered the rolling hills of Ohio. Up the center of the building is a gigantic stone chimney that gave each of the inn's ten rooms its own fireplace. The walls are covered with well-worn black oak, hickory, and cherry paneling. Whoever built the inn also built some mysteries into it.

*The Millfield Inn, in the 1800s, was the hub of life in the Ohio Valley. Now it shelters rats, bats and ghosts.*

# A SECRET ROOM

Up in the attic, next to the chimney, is a secret trap door in the floor. When it is lifted, a secret room about five feet square is revealed. Back in the 1850s, the inn was a stop on the Underground Railroad. People escaping slavery in the South were hidden in this secret room so that they could rest on their journey to Canada. The identity of these brave souls is a secret known only to them. It's a secret that was taken to their graves.

In 1857, a slave known only as Luther was trying to make his way to the inn. He had escaped from a cotton plantation in Alabama and had eluded the bounty hunters for days. Unfortunately, his luck ran out when he reached Ohio. Slave hunters chased him through the brush, wildly shooting their 12-gauge shotguns. Luther managed to escape from the hunters, but was shot in the thigh.

When he finally reached the inn, the innkeeper hid him in the secret attic room. Luther's wound was banaged, and he was given some grog and a hot meal. His wound became infected, however, and several days later he died.

But Luther did not die a peaceful death. His pain and his anger drove him mad. Days after his death, the ghost of Luther was seen staggering through the nearby fields, dressed in rags and dragging the bloody stump of his shot-off leg. To this very day, people say they sometimes see Luther, wandering by the light of the moon, looking for those slave hunters, seeking his revenge before he can rest from his earthly troubles.

## THE BOOTLEGGER'S GHOST

By the 1920s, the Millfield Inn was converted to a private home. One of the people who lived there became yet another ghost of the Millfield Inn — the drunken ghost of Bootlegger Sam. During the 1920s, it was illegal to buy alcohol in America. Overnight, thousands of people started making their own. Sometimes they sold it, sometimes they traded it for eggs and meat. Sam was one of those bootleggers.

Sam had the bright idea of walling in a corner of his living room. If you were inside the house, you couldn't see that there was a secret room. From the outside, everything looked normal. The only way into the room was through a trap door in the basement. Inside the hidden room, Sam built a still.

Day after day, Sam brewed his own corn liquor in that secret room. Sometimes the sheriff would pass by and smell the corn mash cooking, but he didn't see any thing unusual.

One afternoon, Sam sampled a little too much of his homemade brew and fell asleep in the corner. The fire under the still raged and pressure built up in the main chambers. The hissing finally woke Sam up, and he lept to his feet to turn down the heat. As soon as he walked over to the still, KABOOM! Twenty gallons of high-grade corn squeezings blew the still — and Sam — to smithereens. Neighbors rushed to put out the fire and the inn was saved. Bits and pieces of Sam were scattered here and there. But Sam's spirit refused to die. Now and then, people passing by the old Millfield Inn smell Sam's corn mash brewing, and they can hear his drunken laughter rousting across the peaceful countryside.

# LONESOME GHOST TOWNS

America has more wilderness areas than almost any other place on earth. Vast, lonely prairies give way to the towering mountains and desolate deserts of the West. Here, humans are dwarfed by Mother Nature in all her glory. In the 1800s, some of the richest mineral veins in the world lay just beneath the rough stone of those western states. There was enough gold, silver, and copper, to make a king weep with joy. During the last century, the hunger for instant wealth turned hundreds of lonely mountain crags into bustling cities overnight.

Towns quickly grew up around the sight of new-found wealth. Gold panners, silver barrons, and copper bosses flocked to these towns. Taverns, barbershops, and dance halls were soon built. Merchants set up shop in tents until lumber could be cut for buildings. Schools, hospitals, jails, and theaters sprung up out of the dust. Some of these towns became the bustling mega-cities of today. Haven't we all heard of Vulture City, Total Wreck, Big Bug, and Tombstone? These are ghost towns.

These are among the hundreds of towns, left to decay beneath the western sun, wind, sand, and snow. When the money ran out, the bustling towns were abandoned as quickly as they had been built. The fickle humans that lovingly carved the cities out of dust were gone with the wind. Left behind were the ghosts of the dead; the men who died when mines collapsed; the dance hall girls who died of fever; the gunslingers whose bodies were drilled full of lead by the sheriff. They're all up in the cemetery on Boot Hill, and they're lonely. But late at night you might hear in the wilderness the laughter and dancing, the gunshots and the weeping. Listen closely, the ghosts are out there!

*There are hundreds of towns long abandoned in America's west.*

Ghost towns like Vulture City, Total Wreck, and Tombstone were at one time bustling cities of the old West. Today they stand abandoned, decaying beneath the western wind and sun.

## CHAPTER 2
## NIGHTMARE ON CHASE STREET

Moving into a haunted house has ruined the dreams of many people when they find that their "dream home" is filled with nightmares. Take the case of Jack and Janet Smurl in West Pittston, Pennsylvania. The Smurls and their four children moved into their home on Chase Street in 1973. They lived a busy, happy life and gave little thought to the odd occurrences in their home. But soon things happened that could not be ignored. One day the television burst into flames. In the following weeks, both the new stove and the new car mysteriously started on fire. The morning after a new bathtub was installed, it was shredded with claw marks as if a crazed, wild beast had attacked it.

By 1977, the Smurls had gotten used to the hauntings, and tried to laugh them off. The toilet flushed when no one was in the room; the radio blared music although it wasn't plugged in; phantom footsteps clunked upstairs; drawers and windows opened; foul odors stunk up the basement.

# THE TERROR GROWS

In 1984, while Janet was ironing in her kitchen, a cloaked, human-shaped form made of rolling black smoke glided by her. A sudden chill and strange odor overpowered her ability to scream. A year later, Janet was asleep when she was pulled from the bed by an invisible fury. Someone, no, something had grabbed hold of her right leg and dragged her across the floor while she shrieked in terror. The stench returned and a horrendous banging in the walls deafened her. Even the family dog was spooked several weeks later when it began yelping in pain as it was flayed with an invisible whip. Something had to be done!

The Smurls contacted Ed and Lorraine Warren, demonologists who were made famous in the book "Amityville Horror." The Warrens worked for free and had helped rid over 3,000 places of ghosts, including the West Point Military Academy in 1973. The Warrens' message is simple: "There is a demonic underworld, and on some occasions it can be a terrifying problem for people."

*The Warrens (demonologists) conduct a seance to rid the Smurl's home of four spirits.*

# A HUNT FOR DEMONS

In a matter of hours, the Warrens had found the source of the Smurls' problems. Four spirits lived in the house. One was a harmless, senile, old woman. The second spirit was an insane, violent, young woman who was able to cause much harm. The third spirit was a shadowy man who seemed dangerous. When it came to the fourth spirit, trouble was brewing. The fourth spirit was a demon who wanted to create chaos and destroy the family. This demon controlled the other spirits.

Ed Warren suspected that the demon had been sleeping for decades but had been awakened by the presence of the Smurls' teen-age daughter. In many cases, demons are brought out by a teen-ager's stormy emotions. That night everyone gathered together to draw the spirits out into the open. Mirrors rattled, the television glowed, and everyone prayed, but the spirits stubbornly remained.

# THE FAILED EXORCISM

Several months later, Jack Smurl was in the shower when he was attacked by a female form who forcefully kissed him! The woman looked to be about 65 years old. She had long, white, scraggly hair, red eyes, and green gums. Some of her teeth were missing and the rest were vampire-like fangs. The hideous ghost vanished, leaving a sticky substance behind.

In February 1986, the frightened and frustrated Smurls called in a Catholic priest to exorcise the demons. After a long session, the spirits seemed put to rest. But they were warned not to celebrate just yet. There is a strong power in the phantom world, and they are not easily put on the run.

Soon, the spirits started their old tricks again. A second and third exorcism was held. Nothing worked, so the Smurls decided to go on a camping trip. But the demons followed them wherever they went. Their camper was haunted, and while Jack was sleeping, his camper bed spun around in a circle and flew up in the air! The Smurls returned home, frustrated and bewildered.

Upon returning home, the family contacted a local reporter, thinking that the publicity would help attract someone who could solve their problems. They were wrong. When the national media got hold of the story, the Smurls had hundreds of reporters camping in their front lawn and calling their house at all hours. Thousands of people who had heard the story created traffic jams driving by the Smurls' home. Day and night, cars full of pointing, gawking people harassed the Smurls. They received threatening phone calls, and people accused them of being demons.

## WHEN WILL IT END?

The haunting of the Smurl house continues to this day. Exorcisms have failed and no one knows how to help the family. Once again it has been proven that the restless dead will never sleep!

# CHAPTER 3
# HAUNTED ENGLAND

The British Isles must be the most haunted place on earth. Maybe it is because many buildings there are anywhere from one hundred to one thousand years old. Because of the excellent record keeping down through the centuries, we know more about the hauntings in Great Britain than almost anywhere else. The island is a ghost hunter's paradise! When looking through the hundreds of books on the subject, it seems that almost every cottage, castle, church, and theater in the British Isles is haunted.

At Fountains Abbey in Yorkshire, monks can still be heard chanting psalms 800 years after their deaths. At Highgate Cemetery in London, mewling cat ghosts wander among the twisted rubble and overgrown vines of the ancient, crumbling graves. On the road near Jervelaux Abbey, the robed ghost of Archbishop Scrope, who was beheaded in 1405, can be seen walking behind a black coffin that is floating above the ground. The archbishop reads from an open book, his head hovering inches above his body.

*By Jervelaux Abbey, near London, England, the headless robed ghost of Archbishop Scrope, has been seen walking around.*

The picturesque town of Robin Hood's Bay is thought to be the birthplace of Robin Hood, the famous outlaw who robbed from the rich and gave to the poor. On dark nights, the ghosts of Robin Hood and his band of Merry Men can be heard jostling through the cobblestone streets. Near the grey and brooding Middleham Castle a skeleton in a black dress has been seen wandering the moors looking for her lost lover.

## WHITBY ABBEY

The majestic ruins of Whitby Abbey stand high above the sea in Yorkshire, England. The abbey was first built in 657 A.D., but was destroyed by the conquering Vikings about two hundred years later. The abbey was rebuilt in 1067, but the original founder, Saint Hilda, never left. Her ghost, wrapped in a shroud, often appears in one of the abbey's highest windows.

*Robin Hood's Bay is thought to be the birthplace of Robin Hood.*

*Whitby Abbey is said to be haunted by Saint Hilda, the original founder.*

Saint Hilda was known for ridding the area of snakes. She is also responsible for another apparition at Whitby Abbey. Legend has it that Hilda would drive snakes over the high cliffs near the abbey. Before the snakes plunged to their deaths in the icy sea, Hilda would chop their heads off with a whip. Since then, a monstrous, hearse-like coach, guided by a headless driver and pulled by four headless horses, has been seen racing along the cliffs and then plunging over the edge into a watery grave.

The most troubled ghost of Whitby Abbey is a young nun who broke her sacred vows for love. Constance de Beverley was in love with a false-hearted knight named Marmion. The church decided to punish Constance for her misdeeds by bricking her up alive in the abbey dungeon wall. Her ghost can be seen on the dungeon stairwell, crying and begging for release.

On Halloween, the bells of Whitby Abbey can be heard ringing under the sea. That is where the bells were dumped in the 16th century during the English Reformation. The roads around Whitby are also said to be haunted by a mischievous ghost named Hob who has a grudge against travelers in the area. Hob makes cars skid into ditches, turns signposts around, and lets the air out of tires. At least that's what the late-night motorists around Whitby Abbey say.

*The Headless Horseman and his four headless horses are the Haunted Legend of Whitby Abbey.*

# CAERPHILLY CASTLE

One of the most impressive castle ruins in Britain is Caerphilly Castle in Wales. The castle was built in 1268, and has been the sight of dozens of attacks from enemies. With its moat and four huge towers, Caerphilly has seen its share of bloody battles and creepy corpses.

Caerphilly has the usual assortment of headless soldiers and phantom armies that one would expect from Britain's second largest castle. But Caerphilly is also home to one of the most feared and dreaded ghosts in Wales: the Hag of the Dribble (also known as gwrach-y-rhibyn in tongue-twisting Welsh.) The specter of the Hag of the Dribble takes the form of a horrible old witch. The hag has long, matted hair, a hooked nose, piercing red eyes, claw-like fingers and a twisted, hunched back. Her arms look like black wings. People run from the sight of the Hag, but hearing her squealing, screeching voice is what people fear the most. If a person hears the blood-curdling scream of the Hag, they will soon be dead. Several families who lived in the castle had seen the Hag prior to the death of their loved ones.

*Caerphilly Castle is home to one of the most dreaded ghosts of Wales, the "Hag of Dribble."*

# THE END?

Well, not quite. The ghosts of our past will always follow us into the future. Tomorrow, today will be yesterday. Today is the birthday of tomorrow's ghosts. Now that we've hunted down a few phantoms, it's your turn to give it a ghost. Happy haunting!

*This mansion in Ohio, near Lake Erie, is said to be haunted.*